AF322666

A TERRIFYING
STORY BY
1901 ™ STUDIOS
THE DESPICABLE DINER

Series Created by: Josh Walton (Mr. 1901)

Story by: Mr. 1901

Written by: Lindsey Peterson

Welcome...

Welcome to 1901 Studios,

I'm Mr. 1901, and I'm here to tell you some stories. We're a new book series by Zellaphant Books and what we really want to know is what you're truly afraid of. These stories come from the deepest and darkest corners imaginable and we're here to unlock some new fears for you. These stories are scary but they're safe for all ages. These stories will terrify but families everywhere can enjoy them together. These stories are horrifying, but you'll come to love us. If you're reading this, you have a unique opportunity presented to you. You've been carefully selected to become a part of the story. You will most likely be safe from the monsters we've created... but we can only go as far as most likely. Be sure to warn as many people as you can about us, about our creatures. There's plenty of scares to go around so don't be afraid to tell your friends, maybe they can help you.

Each book is intended to be made into a horrifying episode for kids and adults alike to be entertained by. We hope you'll join us. Watch out for new releases of books, stickers, t-shirts and more that we are making, just for you.

Keep your eyes peeled (our monsters *love* peeled eyes) for our 1901 Studios Scary Box Set. Each book is going to have it's very own and you will receive a collectible item from the story the box set is based on. Everything else inside.. well, let's just say it's sure to be a scream. Thank you for reading 1901 Studios and we look forward to seeing you.

Just one last thing:

Don't look behind you.

1901 Studios
An original series by Zellaphant Books

Collect all 10 books in Series One

Follow Us on Instagram:

@ZellaphantBooks
@1901stories

Get more of 1901 Studios by visiting
ZellaphantBooks.com or scanning the QR code
below.

Every book sale is a donation to animals in need

1

Jacob Wallace opened a bleary eye and stared at the sunlight filtering in through the dirty curtains over his window. He wondered what day it was, and what time it was. Judging by the angle of the sun, somewhere between ten and noon. He sat up, opening and closing his mouth again and again in an effort to get rid of the nasty overnight taste. When had he fallen asleep? How had he even made it to his bed?

As he swung his legs over the side of the bed and stretched, he remembered. It was Thsgiving. He'd been up late the night before watching his favorite true crime show, but instead of falling asleep on the couch like he normally did, he managed to get to bed before passing out.

His stomach howled at him as he stood up, making him wonder when he'd last eaten. Jacob spent most of his time watching TV, since there wasn't much else to do. As he stumbled slowly to the bathroom, he tried to remember the last time he'd picked up any groceries. Had it been just a few days ago? Or maybe a week? He couldn't remember. It was hard to remember details like that anymore.

As he closed the medicine cabinet and began brushing his teeth, he looked up into the mirror. A thin, pale face stared back at him. He wondered when he had gotten so thin, and why he had such big purple shadows under his eyes. Jacob felt a twinge of discomfort. He hadn't always been like this...had he? He brushed his teeth and shrugged to himself, figuring he just needed more sleep. That was it. Sleep, and maybe some food later.

As he tried to climb back into bed, though, his stomach reminded him once more that it needed food. The way it was grumbling, he wasn't going to get any rest anytime soon. With a sigh, he shuffled towards the kitchen to see what he could scavenge.

It was times like these that he really missed his mom's cooking. She made a mean lasagna, with homemade sauce and ground beef seasoned with onion and garlic. He missed her desserts the most, lemon meringue pie with a mountain of whipped meringue on top, black forest cake with tart cherries in a bright red glaze, apple pies stuffed with about six apples and baked to a crispy, gooey, cinnamon seasoned perfection...

The thought was making him drool. Turning his attention back to the tiny kitchen of his apartment, he opened the pantry and scanned the contents. Nothing but a canister of salt, some crusty old tortilla chips that looked as if they'd expired in the sixties, and a few packets of sugar. Jacob made his way to the fridge, not feeling much hope. Sure enough, there was nothing in the fridge but some curdled milk and a shriveled old tomato. The rest of the cupboards were bare, too. There was absolutely nothing edible in the whole place.

"Time for some take-out, I guess," he grumbled to himself. There was a Chinese place just down the road from him. He was there so much that Cheng, the head chef, knew him by name. Jacob made his way slowly back to his room, his bad leg paining him a bit as he did so. He'd finished physical therapy over six months ago, but it hadn't really made a difference. The limp was always there, no matter what he did or how much time passed.

Rummaging through his sock drawer, he found his lucky pair of socks, black with Homer Simpson's head printed all over them. Unrolling them, he reached inside one and pulled out a crumpled twenty-dollar bill that had clearly seen better days. It had multiple tears, and the green paper had faded until it looked almost gray, but it would still work. Money was money, after all. Putting the bill in the front pocket of his flannel shirt, Jacob pulled on a coat and started towards the door. Just as he put his hand on the handle, though, the phone rang.

Limping over, he snatched up the receiver. "Hello?"

"Jacob? It's mom."

Inwardly, Jacob felt a slight pang. His parents were both stuck in his native Michigan. Temperatures had already dropped below freezing there, and sheets of snow were tearing their way across the roads between Iowa and Michigan. There was no way his parents could come out here, and no hope of him going out there, either.

"Hi, mom. How are you holding up in that storm out there?"

She sighed. "We're alright, just missing you. How are you holding up?"

"Oh, you know, I'm fine," he lied. His stomach chose that moment to let out a particularly loud grumble. He hoped she couldn't hear the noise over the phone.

"Have you got somewhere to eat? Maybe with a friend or something?"

Jacob twirled the phone cord around his finger until it started to turn blue, then unwound it again. "Uh, maybe. A couple buddies and I were thinking of getting together."

Another lie. He didn't have any friends, and probably wouldn't make any soon. Or ever, for that matter.

"Well, I guess that's good. It's just not the same as being with family, but that makes me feel better knowing you have someone."

He sniffled and shuffled from foot to foot, unsure what to say. "Yep, it should be fine. Are you and dad staying home or going to Grandma's?"

She heaved another sigh. "This storm has gotten pretty bad. We'll probably just have a quiet day today, and celebrate with them on Sunday when things calm down."

"That's good."

A note of concern crept into her voice. "How are things at school? Are your classes manageable?"

He cleared his throat. "Uh, yeah. Glad to have a break, though."

His stomach gave another vicious growl. "Uh, mom, I should probably go. I need to free up the line in case my friends call."

"Okay," she said, the disappointment clear in her voice. "Give us a call later this weekend if you can."

Jacob picked up the phone again, thinking maybe he'd just order over the phone. The snow had begun to fall more heavily, and the thought of being out in it made him shiver. He dialed the number for the Chinese place, expecting the usual busy signal, but to his surprise, he got the voicemail. Hanging up, he picked up the receiver and called again, wondering if it was a random fluke, but it wasn't. House of China was closed for Thanksgiving, which made no sense since Cheng and his family didn't really celebrate Thsgiving. Jacob remembered specifically reading the sign that said they were open seven days a week, year-round, even on Christmas. So why had they closed?

Frustrated, Jacob ambled to the pantry to find the list of fast-food places and their phone numbers that he'd taped there months back. Dialing one after another, he got answering machine after answering machine. At least those places being closed made more sense. He looked up the local grocery store's number and tried that too, to no avail. Everything was closed for Thanksgiving.

"Of course, they are," he muttered angrily. He slumped down into a kitchen chair, wondering what to do next, when the yellow pages caught his eye. Someone had delivered them about a month back to every apartment, and most people had just left them outside.

Picking it up, he flicked through the pages to the restaurant section and moved his finger down the list, praying that at least one of these places would be open. He was starting to get dizzy from hunger.

Almost immediately, he opened the pages to the restaurant guide. That almost never happened. He grinned, hoping that meant that luck was with him and he'd find somewhere that was open. If he couldn't find a place to eat, he was getting increasingly worried about what might happen to him.

2

When Jacob was honest with himself, he didn't really use the yellow pages much except to prank call people when he was bored. With no school and no work to occupy himself, he'd resorted to making the silly calls, laughing himself into hysterics. Now, though, he actually needed the pages, and hoped they could help him.

Initially, Jacob had moved out to Iowa for college. He'd wanted to study architecture, and things had started out well enough. But now things were different. Jacob had been too ashamed to admit that he'd dropped out of school, so he managed on the money his parents sent him for tuition, though the guilt twisted his gut from time to time.

His immediate hunger managed to stave off the guilt this time. As he scanned the list of restaurants in town, Jacob frowned. There were a whole slew of Chinese places, including the one down the street. The city was filled with a good amount of Mexican food places, too, but Mexican food this early in the morning didn't sound great. Who would be open on Thanksgiving? Burger joints? Pizza places?

With an aggravated growl, Jacob started calling place after place after place. To his surprise and dismay, everything was closed, but why? If it had been Christmas, he could understand. That was the biggest holiday in the country, but Thanksgiving wasn't that big of a deal. Most major retailers stayed open on Thanskgiving, so why had everyone just decided to close this year?

Growing desperate, Jacob scanned further down the list, looking for something that wasn't Burger King or Pizza Hut. At last, his finger landed on the word *diner*.

"The desp...hang on a minute."

Squinting harder at the tiny black text, Jacob re-read the words. "Oh, the Delicious Diner."

He chuckled. "Diners are always open! Perfect."

Picking up the phone again, he dialed and waited for several rings. The ringing went on for an unusually long time, so he figured the place just didn't have a message machine set up. As he was about to hang up, though, a voice suddenly answered.

"Hello! You've reached the Delicious Diner, serving up delicious fare seven days a week, all year long! Come on down for amazing breakfast platters of eggs, bacon, pancakes, sausage, and more! Breakfast is served all day long, folks! Don't forget to try our lunch specials like the Ultra Cheddar Burger with seasoned fries, or the spaghetti with giant meatballs!"

The voice on the recording sounded almost like an old-fashioned auctioneer, speaking fast to tell all of the food's admirable qualities, as if it were being sold for charity. The quality of the recording sounded a little off, too. It was tinny, like those old movies from way back in the thirties and forties when sound recording was still new. It was weird, but who cared? It sounded like they had a ton of food on hand.

"...amazing, sizzling steaks cooked right on our grill! Pair it with our homemade garlic mashed potatoes for a match made in heaven! And for dessert, blueberry or strawberry rhubarb cobbler with vanilla ice cream made right here in our old-fashioned ice cream churn..."

Jacob groaned, his stomach feeling as if it was twisting in on itself. "Come on, dude, get to the address! Tell me where this place is!"

He'd noticed that the listing didn't have an address like all the other restaurants did, so he was hoping the message would give an address at some point. After a full ten minutes of rambling about food, way more time than the average message machine could hold, the speaker finally got to location details.

"Now, we are open, folks! You can find us along I-35, between NE 118th and NE 126th. Look for the old road!"

Jacob frowned. The old road? What did that mean? He'd been up and down I-35 several times before and had never seen any "old road." There was just Four Mile Creek and a housing estate out that way. It was pretty desolate, mostly country. With a shrug, he got up and moved towards the door, figuring the place must have been built recently. That would explain the long-winded message on the phone. He grabbed his keys and coat once again and made his way down the stairs to the parking lot.

As he drove slowly on the I-35 in the direction of the old abandoned high school campus, he scanned the side of the road to the left and right, seeing nothing but the flat, green landscape that made up most of the state. There were certainly no signs advertising the place, and no old road. Figuring he'd gotten it wrong or missed the diner, he turned and went back the other way until he reached NE 118th. Nothing.

As Jacob turned around once again, he realized he hadn't driven all the way to NE 126th, so he turned around again and made his way along the road at twenty miles an hour, looking for any odd roads or dirt paths that might lead to the diner. Finally, as he was nearing 126th, he caught sight of a tiny dirt road that looked like no more than a cow path. He stopped the car and peered out the window, his eyes following the dirt trail back to a grove of trees and brush.

He saw a small, ramshackle building nestled among the brush that he swore wasn't there before. A long drive of cracked, dirty pavement led from the cow path to the diner. It looked like it was maybe half a mile down the path. With a shrug, urged on by his groaning stomach, he turned and made his way up the path. The car protested a little on the dirt path, wobbling along the rutted track at five miles an hour. The path crossed the creek, and someone had put down a bridge of sorts, which was little more than a few two-by-fours nailed together. Jacob stopped the car and leaned out, seriously thinking about turning around right then.

With a nervous gulp, he lined up his tires with the bridge and crossed, praying the entire way. The old planks held and he reached the point where the pavement began. It was actually part of a small parking lot, and looked even worse up close. It was pocked here and there with potholes, and clearly hadn't been maintained in the last twenty years at least.

The building itself looked like little more than a shack, with siding that had once been white, but now hovered between gray and pale yellow. Trees surrounded the little building, making it hard to see even when you were up close. Jacob realized that unless you knew what to look for, the average customer would miss the place completely.

"That's weird. You'd think if it was a new place, they'd want to make themselves known a little better. I guess maybe it's not new after all."

The lack of address, the strange recording, the out of the way location, all started to make the hair on the back of Jacob's neck rise. Why would someone want to build a restaurant way out here, far from the main road? He was starting to have second thoughts.

Still, he was starving, and this was the only place that was open. Hunger won out in the end, so he parked next to the shabby looking building. There was a large bay window at the front of the building, with letters that must have once glowed neon above it. The only two discernable letters were "D" and "E," both of which were in "Delicious Diner," so Jacob knew he had the right place.

As he stared at the old building, feeling a little dubious, he reasoned that these little mom and pop places probably focused on the interior of the building most. Maybe once the place picked up a bit, the owner would work on the exterior when there was more time and money. Yeah, that was it. Small restaurants were always like this, shabby and worn on the outside, but okay on the inside. And a lot of times, the food was great.

There was absolutely nothing to worry about. At least, that's what Jacob told himself.

3

As Jacob peered through the filthy window at the front of the restaurant to the interior, he wondered how many people had come to this diner over the years. Had the place been a lot busier back when it first opened? Was that the reason for the long phone message, to try to draw people in?

Maybe families used to come here with their small children, stopping at the diner on the way to a fun vacation. Or perhaps truckers stopped here for lunch or dinner on a long, lonely run. Maybe there had been people here like him, alone on holidays, wondering what to do with themselves when they had nobody to celebrate with.

He thought about all those people, wondered if they had been frightened of the world around them, or intrigued by it. Had they observed the changes in the world with fear or fascination? Maybe two young kids had their first date here, or a bitter couple their last as they tried to save the dying embers of their marriage. Were the people who had visited this diner before gone? Or were they still living?

Jacob shook his head, chuckling. "I must really be hungry and losing it. Who knows how long this place has been around? It's so out of the way, probably nobody has been here in a while. That's why I didn't notice it before."

And yet, he couldn't quite shake the fact that the diner was ancient. If no one came here anymore, how was the place still in business? He didn't know much about running a small business, but it was bound to be expensive. The building had obviously been around for years, and as he peered inside, he could tell that the fixtures and furniture dated at least back to the 1950s.

Again, he wondered how he had never seen this place before. Why wasn't the address listed in the yellow pages if it had been here since the fifties? Most businesses advertised relentlessly, to the point of being annoying. The goal was always to draw more business, so how did this place even function anymore? It made no sense at all.

"I've got to eat something," he muttered to himself, shaking his head. "I'm just imagining things, getting worked up over nothing. Maybe someone rich owns it, and they can afford to just let it sit and wait for customers."

He knew it wasn't the truth. A rich person would invest in a business to make more money, not just let it randomly sit. Still, beggars couldn't be choosers. He needed food, any food.

As Jacob moved closer to the building, though, a vague sense of unease gripped him. There was just...something off about this place. He couldn't quite put a finger on the exact emotion, but it landed somewhere between wariness and that queasy feeling you get when you've eaten too much melted cheese.

But why should he be afraid of a diner? It was probably the most holey hole in the wall place he'd ever seen, and he'd been to some really nasty places before. This one took the cake, but the food might still be okay. His stomach twisted at the thought of something deep-fried in lard or vegetable oil or whatever they used.

Taking a deep breath, Jacob took a few more steps towards the door, then hesitated. That *not right* feeling struck again, on a deeper level this time. He wondered if this was the kind of feeling a gazelle got when drinking at a pond or watering hole where crocodiles were known to lurk. All the serial killer specials he'd watched on TV flashed through his mind, making him wonder if this was all a clever trap set up to lure in innocent victims. A person would have to be really hungry or really stupid to walk into such a trap. Jacob was definitely hungry, and he wondered about the stupid sometimes.

As he sat there deliberating, staring at the ancient, crusty door, the wind began to pick up. It was the type of wind to cut through whatever clothing you were wearing, even if you had the thickest, most expensive snow gear.

Jacob began to shiver. Iowa wasn't too much different weather wise from Michigan, but the frustrating thing about Iowa was the wind. Being a prairie state, wind just raced across the fields with nothing to break its momentum. The wind could bring the air temperature down as much as ten degrees, sometimes more.

He turned and looked longingly back at his car. The heater wasn't great, but it worked. Should he go back? Then again, if he got in his car, there was no hope of food. Everything was closed down for Thanksgiving. He'd just have to go to his apartment and wait the hunger out until tomorrow.

The wind continued to bite into him, and with it came flurries of new snow. He looked up at the sky, despairing, then back at the door before him. "I've got to eat. The sooner the better so I can get out of this weather."

Yes, he'd just go get a quick meal. Maybe even order it to go so he could get out of there faster. It would be fine. Everything would be fine.

Jacob repeated the mantra to himself as he grasped the door and pulled. The door screeched like an unholy demon, raising the hairs on the back of his neck. It seemed like the door was glued to the pavement below it, holding onto the cement for dear life as if it really didn't want to be opened. It became a sort of tug-of-war with the door, a back-and-forth screeching, grinding motion that eventually made enough of a crack for Jacob to slip through.

He emerged into the dining room, if you could call it that, and shuddered. The air in here was cold, too, so he fought another vicious tug-of-war with the door, forcing it closed against the sharp wind. That ominous feeling gripped him again as the door finally slammed into place. Would he be able to get out again?

Shaking the fears out of his mind, he turned and looked around the room once more. The booths had once been striped a bright red and white, but were now covered with a dingy coat of dust and cobwebs, some of them thick enough to look like tablecloths. Whoever had eaten here last had left plates of food on some of the tables, and most of it had rotted.

Where were the cooks and the waiters? Where was the host or hostess? When had this place even opened? Or, for that matter, when had it closed? Had someone abandoned it? Or was it just closed? Maybe he'd gotten the message machine in error.

As Jacob surveyed the room, he noticed a large sign very close to the front door. It was almost freakishly tall, with a white background and lettering in chipped black paint that read *Seat yourself where you find a menu.*

"What on earth does that mean?" Jacob wondered aloud. "The waiter is supposed to bring you a menu. This place is weird."

Still, he stood by the door, too nervous to move. He didn't want to follow the signs directions. He was the only customer, and he knew he'd feel better if he could talk to someone.

"Hello?" he called. "Is anyone here?"

Silence. His heart hammering, Jacob scooted past the sign and walked a little further in. Maybe whoever worked here was at the far back of the building. They probably hadn't heard him come in, even though the door's screeches could have raised the dead.

"Hello?" he called again, his voice starting to sound strained. "I called and got the message that you guys still serve food. Is this the Delicious Diner?"

Still nothing. Now that he was in here, Jacob couldn't stand the thought of going back outside. The storm was picking up, the small flurries from before now turning into large, fluffy flakes. They were blowing sideways past the window. Jacob shuddered, and turned back to the interior.

"Is anyone here?" he hollered at the top of his lungs. "I was hoping to grab some lunch!"

Maybe that was it. They just hadn't opened yet. A lot of restaurants did that. But then Jacob remembered the phone message talking about breakfast. If they served breakfast, then surely they were open by now. The door hadn't been locked, either.

With no other choice, Jacob stepped further inside to explore the old diner and see if he could find someone to help him.

4

As he wandered through the dining area, Jacob realized that he was still freezing. The air inside seemed to be just as cold as outside, even without the wind blowing. In fact, it felt even a little colder. He pulled his jacket more tightly around him, wishing that he'd brought his heavier winter coat with the hood. Though the idea of exploring didn't really appeal to him, he knew he had to do something. At this point, standing still wasn't a good idea.

Passing the ripped and faded booths, the cracked, plasticky tablecloths with plates of rotting food on them, Jacob realized he needed to keep an eye out for critters. This far out from town and in weather like this, a dilapidated old building such as this one would be open game for racoons, rats, mice, chipmunks, and squirrels. He shuddered as he wondered if he was stepping in their waste right now.

The more he wandered, the more he thought about what had happened here. Why would people just leave? Under his wary feeling, Jacob also felt a sense of curiosity. Food still sat on the tables, moldering and grimy. Why would people just leave their meals behind? Had something catastrophic happened? Did the food make them sick? Maybe there had been a fire in the kitchen, or a car hit the restaurant or something. Then again, the place was old and dilapidated, but Jacob couldn't see any burns or shattered glass anywhere.

As he had the thought, he realized that the large bay window at the front of the building seemed to be the only one. Some tiny square windows were on the side walls at opposite ends of the building, but they were more like the kind of windows you'd see in a bathroom, small and high up on the wall. Jacob wondered wildly how he would get out if something happened and he had to escape. The glass in the bay window was thick and likely hard to break, but there was no hope of crawling out of one of those tiny windows, either. The realization gave him a crawling sense of claustrophobia. He turned back to the door, wondering if it was a good idea to just try to get out of there.

A sudden scraping noise made him jump. He hurried back to the front door as fast as he could on his bad leg, his heart thundering in his chest. When he'd had a few moments to calm down, he tried to think of logical explanations. Maybe it was just some critters trying to find refuge in the creepy old place. Maybe it was someone who worked here.

Or it could be something more sinister…

"Stop being stupid," he ordered himself. "It's probably nothing. There's nothing to worry about."

Jacob stood still, trying to hear the noise again over the pounding of his heart. He turned his head quickly. There it was again. *Scritch scratch, scritch scratch.* He scanned the room again, paying attention to even the smallest details. Under the scratching noises, he thought he detected a few faint notes. It was music!

He heaved a sigh of relief. It must be a jukebox. All these old diners seemed to have one. Moving back through the dining room, he rounded a partition wall and saw it, nestled against the far back wall of the other room. Like everything else, it looked as if it belonged in the 1950s. The design was different from the kind of Jukeboxes Jacob had seen before, and he realized it must have been one of the first models. Rather than a rounded top with flashing neon lights, this one was made of a sort of metal frame, the top covered in glass so a person could look inside and choose a record. The selection buttons were just below it, offering only about twenty songs. A small wooden cabinet was on the front near the middle. Jacob didn't know whether the doors were some sort of access panel to fix the inner workings, or if it was some kind of storage space.

As he moved his eyes towards the glass panel, the lights inside of it flickered faintly. The song was scratchy and indistinct because the warped record inside wobbled to and fro like a drunken sailor. Jacob was surprised it still worked. He looked around, noting that none of the lights or other electrics in the place seemed to work. As he gazed down at the machine, he reckoned that the wiring in the old place probably still worked, and that the lights were on a separate circuit to the Jukebox. He wouldn't let his mind dream up any other explanation.

Despite his self-reassurances, the hairs on the back of Jacob's neck rose once more as the song continued to play. It was one of those old-timey songs from the forties or whatever that kind of just played the same wordless melody over and over again, but there was something sinister about it, some melancholic undertones or a minor key that just didn't quite sound right. Something about the melody jangled Jacob's nerves.

The song ended, and another one came on, a slightly more upbeat tune with words this time. As if he was mesmerized, Jacob crept closer to the machine, trying to make out the garbled words. He could only catch the occasional word, a *come on down* here, or a *ours is the best* there. The tune and lyrics reminded Jacob vaguely of the message machine with the cheery male voice. In fact, he could have sworn that the voice in the jukebox and the voice on the phone were one and the same.

Before he knew it, Jacob was standing right next to the jukebox, leaning closer to try to make out the words. A long melody played and the singer stopped. Jacob pounded against the selection keys in frustration. If he could only hear the song, maybe he'd find out what was going on here, why this place had been deserted, why no one seemed to be working.

To his surprise, the warbly, staticky sound stopped and the recording became clear. He realized that the song really did have the same words as the phone recording, talking about tasty breakfast dishes, lunch specials, and sizzling steaks for dinner. As the song continued, though, Jacob began to hear other things. The singer seemed to mention something about never leaving a place, but what place? The recording faded out once more, so he slammed his fist against the selection keys. Same as before, the recording became sharp again and started to rise gradually in volume.

"Our customers are delicious, the younger the more nutritious. Who will be your appetizer, don't ask questions, be none the wiser."

Jacob stepped back as if he'd been bitten by a spider, his heart pounding wildly once more. "Did that song just say what I thought it said?"

His heart pounding, he took another few steps back. He shook his head, his fingertips brushing against his forehead. He felt a little lightheaded, though from hunger or fear, he wasn't sure.

"No, no, this is crazy. I'm just super hungry and imagining things. I'm sure he said that our *food* is delicious...there's no way he said *who* instead of *what*."

As the weird song continued, the voice grew deeper, more sinister, taking on that same strange minor key as the song before. Jacob stepped back even further, telling himself over and over that he was imagining it. He had to be. There was no other explanation. Though he tried to move, he felt as if his legs had been glued to the floor. The voice in the jukebox went from growling to screeching, a high-pitched keening scream that set Jacob's nerves on fire, getting louder and louder with each passing second.

5

In addition to the unnerving screaming, a scraping, grinding sound started coming from inside the machine. Jacob backed up again, only to find that he was standing against the far wall and couldn't get any further away from the psychotic machine. Was the whole thing was about to blow?

Something was clearly wrong with the Jukebox, but what? Dust and grime coated every surface of the old machine, so it was probably gumming up the inner workings, too. But would it really make the singer's voice start screaming like that? Jacob had never heard of a record malfunctioning like that. Maybe the gummed-up works was causing the concrete scraping sound. The sound seemed to enter into every particle of Jacob's body, making him tense up and press the heels of his hands to his ears. It had to stop. It had to!

The screaming only got louder, threatening to burst Jacob's eardrums with the throbbing noise. His fear slowly morphed to anger and frustration. Jacob dropped his hands from his ears and headed for the machine. If it was making noises like this, then he had to unplug it. That was the only way to get it to stop.

He recalled an old alarm clock he'd used when he was in middle school. After a number of years, it had started screeching at odd times when it hadn't been set, and the clock was always off by several minutes one way or another. Anytime it had started acting up, he'd simply unplugged it and it solved the problem.

Just like the door, though, the Jukebox seemed to be glued to the floor when Jacob tried to move it forward. He pushed against it without much luck. The thing weighed a ton, and he was already so hungry that his limbs felt weak and a sweat broke out on his forehead after only a few pushes. How was this thing still running after so many years? And how was it so heavy?

At long last, he managed to jerk the Jukebox forward enough to reach back behind it. The space behind it was filled with who knew how many years of grease and dust bunnies, but Jacob didn't care. He'd do anything to get the screaming to stop. He spotted a huge old black cord and gave it an almighty yank, expecting resistance from what was probably an archaic old electrical socket. Instead, he flew back and landed on his bottom, the cord clutched tightly in his hand. The stupid thing wasn't even plugged in!

Jacob dropped the cord the way he'd drop a scorpion, then scooted back along the filthy floor several feet. The screaming from the Jukebox continued to grow louder and louder, rattling the moldy old cups on the tables and the glass in the large bay window. How could it function when it wasn't even plugged in? Jacob began to shake uncontrollably, his chest heaving with each breath.

"Stop it!" Jacob hollered. He got to his feet, his fists clenched. "Shut up, you stupid old thing!"

Predictably, the screeching, wailing awfulness only got louder. The singer wasn't even saying words anymore, just screaming at the top of his lungs like a banshee. As the shrieking continued, a sound like a shovel scraping against concrete began alongside it, making the insides of Jacob's skull rattle around. The noises then started coming in short bursts, alternating screaming with concrete scraping. Jacob's head pounded with the worst headache he'd ever had in his life.

"Stop!!!" Jacob hollered again. "Make it *stop*!"

He had no idea who he was yelling at, or why he was yelling, except that the pain in his head was becoming unbearable. Even more than food in that moment, he wanted an ibuprofen to ease the ache in his head. With an almighty roar, he rushed at the Jukebox and body slammed it like a linebacker in a football game. A jolt of pain shot through his shoulder at the contact, but the pulsing adrenaline in his system dulled it.

Rearing back, Jacob ran for the Jukebox again, wrapping his arms around it this time and hauling it sideways with all his might. The machine tipped forward, the wobbly screams and scrapes now at a pitch so high that Jacob heard glasses shattering in the dining room. With a guttural roar and another heave, the Jukebox toppled, the glass smashing all over the floor, the wood cabinetry caving inward on itself.

The screams and scrapes stopped abruptly, plunging Jacob and the entire diner into an eerie silence. Jacob's ears still rang from the screeches as he stared down at the Jukebox, but the silence was a blessed relief. His arms and back were sore, and his head still pounded, but he felt oddly victorious, as if he'd single-handedly taken down a grizzly bear. The thought bolstered him a little, his shaking subsiding.

Stepping closer, he gave the side of the Jukebox a small kick, almost as if he was checking to see if it was dead. The machine made no noise. Jacob took several deep breaths, then crossed his arms around his thin torso. The temporary rush of adrenaline was gone. The sweat he'd built up trying to topple the machine now made him feel colder than ever. He pulled his jacket around him as tightly as it would go, but nothing seemed to ward off the chill.

More than ever, he just wanted to get out of this place. His hunger forgotten, he turned to the partition wall and went through the arch to the other part of the dining room, making for the door. He supposed he'd just go hungry today. It was really his only choice. No one had been in this diner for years. The message machine was some kind of screw up.

Jacob was almost to the front door when he heard the sound. It was faint, far away from the front door of the diner, but Jacob knew that sound. It was a ding, like a small bell would make when an order was ready to be picked up. How many times had he been in restaurants and heard a ding like that? He'd know it anywhere.

Far from being comforting, the noise only set Jacob more on edge. Slowly, dreading what he would see, Jacob walked towards the small window in the wall where orders would be given out to the waiter or waitress from the kitchen. When he looked, however, there was nothing. Not even a bell on the windowsill for the cook to whack with a spatula. Then what had made the sound?

He slowly approached the counter with the row of stools. Maybe someone had set a bell down behind the countertop years ago and something had fallen on it. Standing on tiptoe, Jacob peered over the edge of the countertop where people used to eat their meals to the space behind, but aside from old bits of paper, there was nothing there.

Jacob swallowed hard as he backed away towards the front door, his throat dry. This place was getting too weird. He knew he *had* to get out. As he walked over to the front door, he saw to his dismay that the storm had grown even worse while he'd been exploring the diner. The window was completely whited out, and from what he could see, a small pile of snow had blown against the door. The stupid thing was already hard to open, but now he'd have to push against several inches of built-up snow. Even powdery snow could get some serious weight when all piled together.

Though he knew it was likely fruitless, he approached the door and gave it a push. It didn't even budge an inch. He tried again, heaving against the door with his full bodyweight, like he'd done with the Jukebox. No luck.

Whether or not he liked it, Jacob was stuck. No matter how big this room is, this building, the claustrophobia was going to set in quickly. There's something terrifying about knowing you may not have anywhere to go. The walls close in on you, a few feet at a time. Breathing gets more difficult as you feel the room getting smaller. It feels like the air is getting sucked out as everything around you shrinks.

If Jacob doesn't find a way out, he's going to be done for.

6

Stunned, Jacob sat down at the booth closest to the front door, his heart pounding hollowly in his chest. How long would this storm go on? How much snow was expected? Without access to a television, he had no idea what the weather was like. All he knew was that it was a blizzard, and that he'd be stuck for some time.

Besides that, no one knew where he was. He didn't talk to his neighbors, and he'd lost his only friend over a year ago. No one knew or cared about him here in his new town, and the only people who did care were a thousand miles away. No one would wonder where he'd gotten off to. He seriously doubted that there was a phone in this disgusting old place, and even if there was, it probably wouldn't work. And even if there was a working phone, who would he call? The police? They'd laugh at him.

Taking a few deep breaths, Jacob tried to think rationally. He just had to wait out the storm, that was all. It couldn't last forever. He'd just wait for a few hours or so, and the storm should clear up enough that he could leave.

Even as he repeated the phrase in his mind, though, he felt hopelessness creeping over him like a shadowy dusk. He'd heard about blizzards like this lasting days, sometimes even up to a week. What if he starved to death by then? If the snow continued to pile up like it was currently doing, that was the most likely scenario.

Jacob drummed his fingers on the table, contemplating trying to force his way out the door again. He'd shoved over a gigantic old Jukebox. How hard could a door be? Sure, it had been hard to get open when he came inside, but maybe it only moved like that one way. Maybe he hadn't pushed in the right spot when he'd tried before. Perhaps the snow had jammed in under the door, making a wedge that could be moved or pushed out.

Even as he had the thoughts, he dismissed them. Whatever energy he had from the adrenaline surge he'd gotten was long gone. He felt completely sapped of strength. He laid his head on the table, despair sinking deep into his bones as he realized again that there was no way out. How had he been so stupid? How had he let it get to this point?

A shuffling noise at his feet made him jerk upright. Who, or *what*, was that? Jacob sat in the crusty old booth, rigid with terror, afraid to move even a single muscle.

"It's just the animals that live in this place," he murmured to himself. "They're scuttling around on the floor down there. Just ignore them. Everything will be fine."

Jacob's wild imagination took off again, and he imagined someone investigating this place and finding him still alive, totally insane, rocking back and forth in this very booth and telling himself that everything would be fine. If by some miracle he lived to get out of this place, he probably would be insane.

Besides, he knew that saying the words over and over again to himself wouldn't make them true. Wasn't that the definition of insanity? Doing the same thing over and over and expecting different results?

The noise sounded again, making Jacob jump. No, this wasn't the small, scratchy noises of an animal burrowing or looking for food or making a nest. It was the sound of moving feet, like a waiter walking around to different tables, checking on patrons and refilling glasses. But no one else was in the diner. Those sounds should have been impossible.

Jacob's hands trembled as he leaned over and peeked under the table. At this point, he would have been relieved to see a red-eyed rat or a rabid racoon because at least that was something explainable. Once again, he saw nothing. At that point, his whole body began to shake again, and not just from the cold. As he sat back up, he gasped and pushed his back hard against the seat of the booth, his heart slamming against his ribcage.

He had to be hallucinating. That was the only explanation.

Sitting atop the table was a tall glass of water next to a menu. The glass was filled to the brim with ice cubes and water, condensation dripping down the sides onto the crusty tablecloth. The front of the menu was plain white and edged with black, no diner logo, no address, no phone number, nothing that a normal menu would have. It was completely blank.

"This is a hallucination. It has to be. I've got hypothermia because it's so cold in here, and I must be in the late stages if I'm imagining stuff like this."

Hearing the words out loud helped Jacob reassure himself, if only a little. Plenty of people got lost out in the cold, even in 1990. It could happen to anyone. At least it would explain all the unnatural things happening in this creepy place. Dying of hypothermia was less humiliating than just going insane, as he'd thought he was before. The thought was only slightly comforting, though. Hypothermia might be a less humiliating death, but he knew from the things he'd learned in school that it could be a long, drawn-out death.

Jacob found himself suddenly wishing for a quick death. Hallucinating and being scared to death wasn't exactly a fun way to spend his last moments. He shook his head, trying to push away the dark thoughts. At least hypothermia was explainable, he reminded himself. It made sense. Because if it wasn't hypothermia causing all these weird things to happen...what was?

Once more, he gave himself a firm, mental shove. None of this was supernatural. It was just his mind playing tricks on him from the extreme cold and hunger he was feeling. That was all. The best thing he could do would be to try to think straight. He had to get his panic down and clear his mind.

As Jacob stared at the cup, he realized that in addition to being hungry and cold, he was also desperately thirsty. Several more beads of condensation ran the length of the cup to the tablecloth, the ice clinking together in the water in such an inviting way. Even if it was all a product of his starved and freezing imagination, maybe drinking some of that water would help pass the time and make him feel a little better. Even if it was tap water, it couldn't be that bad. It was what he drank at home.

He reached out and touched the glass. The cup felt cold in his hands, an unwelcome feeling in the already freezing diner, but the thought of ice water on his parched throat kept his hand firmly clutched around the glass. Lifting it, Jacob brought it to his lips and took a big chug, only to then spew the water across the table, coughing and spluttering. He slammed the glass down on the table and screamed as the water splashed out of the glass and scalded his hands.

Though the water looked cold and icy, it had burned a searing path down his lips, tongue, and throat, as if he'd been drinking boiling water, or even lava. Clutching at his coat, Jacob used it to wipe the still burning water from his mouth and hands, wondering with a terrifying jolt if he'd been given some kind of acid. Was that how he was going to die in this horrible place, by drinking acid? Maybe whoever had given him the glass thought they were doing a kindness, making Jacob's death quick. Even if that was the point, it certainly wasn't a kindness. Jacob realized now that he didn't want a slow death or a quick death. He didn't want to die at all, but it seemed like the diner had other plans.

7

The thought of dying by acid ingestion scared Jacob more than anything else that day had. What kind of maniac had thought it would be funny to burn his mouth and body like that? And if they thought they were helping, then whoever it was had come unhinged.

When the hot liquid didn't melt the fabric of his coat or sizzle when it came in contact with the water, though, Jacob realized it couldn't be acid. He knew he'd be in way worse shape if it really had been acid. But how was icy water so *hot*? It was impossible!

Reaching out a tentative hand, Jacob touched the glass again. It was still cold to the touch, just like before. Withdrawing his fingers, he wiped them hurriedly on his coat just in case the condensation on the outside of the glass grew hot. Again, his fear grew into intense anger. He clenched his teeth, his rage getting the better of him.

"Is this some kind of sick joke?" he yelled, feeling even more irritated when his voice squeaked up an octave on the last word. "If so, it's not funny anymore! In fact, none of it's funny!"

Just then, he noticed a blurry green shape in the glass that he hadn't seen before. Rotating the glass around so that the green part was facing him, he saw a logo for the diner inscribed on the side in vivid green letters outlined in purple. Underneath the words was a green anchor, also outlined in purple.

The Despicable Diner

"Well, that's one thing that's right about this place," Jacob muttered, his tone disgusted. "This place really *is* despicable. And disgusting, and dirty, and horrible, and messed up, and STUPID!"

Saying those things felt good, but Jacob knew they wouldn't fix anything. Raging about everything going wrong wasn't the way to solve a problem. He urged himself once more to think, to not give in to panic, to find a way *out*.

In the following silence, another ding sounded, as if an order was ready for pickup. Once again, it seemed to come from the small window to the kitchen, even though there was no one there, and no bell. Jacon shook his head, his anger growing even more. Someone was messing with him, and now he really wanted to find out who it was.

Rising slowly to his feet, Jacob made his way towards the kitchen and the small order window. As he approached the ancient counter, covered with what looked like decades of grime, he peered into the dark space behind the window. In the dimness, he could just barely make out the outline of a door. Was it a door into the kitchen from the diner? Or did the door lead outside? Either way, it was a possibility.

As he had the thought, Jacob felt an ominous feeling in the pit of his stomach, much like the feeling he'd gotten when he was standing outside the diner. The last thing he wanted to do was explore the kitchen. His gut practically screamed at him not to do it. The diner itself was already bad enough, and the kitchen could be much worse, but what else could he do? Besides, moving around might help with the growing numbing sensation in his fingers and toes. He'd read or heard somewhere that sitting down and especially getting sleepy were really bad signs when it came to hypothermia.

So, with dread-filled steps, he shuffled around the edge of the front counter, trying not to touch whatever sticky grime had taken up residence there. It was hard not to cringe as he climbed over crates of broken milk bottles, egg cartons with blackened, cracked eggs, and a trash can full of rotted food so disgusting that it didn't even stink. It must have been there so long that it lost its stench long ago.

Now that he had a better look behind the counter, Jacob saw that it wasn't just papers littering the back area of the counter. Large piles of what looked like gummy ketchup and mustard covered the surface. Paper napkins, ed with age and stained with food, littered the entire surface. Crumbs, dust bunnies the size of softballs, bread that was black from mold, broken glass all mixed in with the debris. Jacob suddenly felt glad that he hadn't been served any food here. Whoever had owned this diner was a real pig. Maybe everyone who'd eaten here had gotten horribly ill, died in their chairs, and their bones turned to dust in the intervening years.

Trying to ignore the churning in his empty stomach, Jacob rounded a corner and saw a door ahead, one that looked like it led into the kitchen. If this door was here, around the corner and out of customer view, then the other door probably led outside to freedom. Jacob's heart lifted at the thought.

And yet, that feeling gripped him again, the feeling that there was something in that kitchen he definitely didn't want to see. And yet, if this was his only chance for freedom, he had to take the chance. Jacob stood there for several minutes, caught between his lurking fear of whatever he might find in that kitchen and his desperate urge to escape and stay alive.

Could the door in the kitchen be a hallucination, too? A vision in his mind that would cause something horrible to happen? Or what if his fear of the kitchen was some sort of weird illusion? What was even real anymore?

Jacob took in several deep breaths. "I'm letting my panic get the better of me again. I've got to stop, I have to think straight, or I'll never get out of here alive."

Nodding to himself, he stepped closer to the door, one foot over the other, wobbling a little on his bad leg. He reached out to touch the door and the feeling grew so intense that he thought he might throw up. Doubling over, he put his hands on his knees, then straightened and tried again. As soon as his fingers touched the door, he began to dry heave. Shaking his head, he stepped back. He'd ignored the feeling outside the diner, and now he was in a terrible mess, so ignoring the feeling now would probably result in his death, or worse.

Jacob gave a growl of frustration and pounded his fist involuntarily on the countertop, causing another ding to sound. Whirling around, he noticed an old-fashioned cash register sitting atop the counter, its massive keys sticking straight up out of a rounded, brown belly of sorts. There was a drawer beneath the cash register belly, and a bell on the side that would have rung each time a transaction was made.

"So, this is where the dinging is coming from," Jacob muttered, feeling a bit foolish for getting so worked up. Peering closely at the machine, he squinted at the tiny glass screen that showed the amount processed from the last transaction. As soon as he saw the numbers, Jacob stepped back and scratched his chin.

"Fifty-five cents? That can't be right. Who would buy something for fifty-five cents? Who would sell something for fifty-five cents?"

Jacob knew he was blabbering, but the sound of his own voice helped to calm his nerves a little. The place had to be positively ancient if people were buying meals for such a low price. As he gazed down at the old machine, he noticed that the button reading SALE wasn't covered in a thick layer of dust, like the other keys. A sweat broke out on his forehead as his heart began to pound. Had the button been pressed recently? If so, by who? Had someone else gotten trapped in this diner? The thought was both terrifying and exhilarating. What if that person had found a way out? Then again, what if the person hadn't escaped, and their remains were still here?

8

His pulse roaring in his ears, Jacob turned this way and that, scanning the floor around him for any sign of bones or other human remains. There was nothing there except the disgusting litter and rotted food, but Jacob still felt on edge. Without a doubt, someone had been here before him. Maybe multiple people. What had happened to them?

Despite the terror rising up inside him, Jacob felt a strong urge to push the button. This whole place was insane. Maybe the contents of the drawer would have some kind of clue. If nothing else, there might even be a little money in there, which would come in handy if he managed to get out of here. Maybe he would learn something about the person or people who had last been here. All he had to do was push one little button.

But what if something awful happened when he pushed the button? The Jukebox had seemed okay until it started screaming at him. He wasn't wild about repeating that experience. But doing nothing was getting him nowhere. He had to try. Taking a deep breath, he rested his forefinger on the SALE button and pushed.

Ding!

Jacob gave an involuntary little nod, his suspicions confirmed. The noises had been coming from this register, and not the kitchen. He felt a sudden surge of gratitude that he hadn't gone into the kitchen, after all. Who knew what kind of bullet he'd dodged?

To his dismay, there was no cash and no coins in the drawer at all. It didn't even look like the typical cash register drawer, with dividers for each type of bill and an open area at the front for coins. The entire drawer was just one large space, filled with all sorts of strange things. It was as if the register acted as a weird filing cabinet or some sort of twisted lost and found. How had these things even gotten in here? When he'd worked at a fast food place in high school, they'd had a designated box under the cash register counter for things people had left behind.

He couldn't imagine why someone would jam the drawer full of all this junk.

Looking down, Jacob began sifting through the dusty items. He saw a couple watches, some rings, even a few video rental membership cards. With shaking fingers, Jacob lifted some of the things out, laying them on the counter next to the register, and left other things inside the drawer. There were movie ticket stubs, tea lights, paper clips, old letters with the names and addresses smeared with water and dust, deflated remains of balloons, marbles, and old pieces of hard candy. It was a strange collection to say the least, even weirder than the junk drawer Jacob had back home in his kitchen.

Among the rubble, he found a license which looked almost new. It had the same plastic finish and background picture as modern licenses, which raised the hairs on the back of Jacob's neck. It had to be the only modern thing in this place, aside from the video rental cards. He read the name on the license.

"Pam," he murmured. Her last name had been scratched off, whether by or on purpose, he wasn't sure. Why did that name ring a bell? He'd heard it somewhere before, he knew, but where? It wasn't a very common name, so he knew he wasn't just imagining things. Glancing over at the picture, he studied what features he could pick out of the woman's face. She had medium brunette hair that hung past her shoulders, a reluctant smile so common to driver's license photos, and wide, brown eyes. Her skin looked tan and smooth. The weirdest thing was that it was an out-of-state license. She was from Wisconsin.

Pam who? The question raced through his mind over and over again. Where had he heard it before? When Jacob moved his eyes over to the identifying information, such as address, license number, and whether she had corrective lenses, he found it had all been scratched off, too. Only her first name and her picture were even slightly distinguishable. Disgusted, Jacob threw the license back down in the drawer and slammed it, making it ding again.

With no other leads to follow or ideas to try, Jacob reluctantly shuffled back to the booth, his head hanging low. All he could do was sit and wait, but wait for what? For someone to come out and serve him? For some sign of life? For the snow to stop? For his eventual death by starvation? The dire thoughts weighed on him as he slumped into the seat at the booth by the door. Propping his elbows on the table before him, he buried his face in his hands.

After a while, he sat up and looked down at the table. The menu still sat there, blank and white and creepy. He hadn't bothered to pick it up when he was sitting there before, but now he wondered if it might be worth a look. Maybe it had some clue as to what had happened in this crazy place.

Though the menu had several pages, all of the offerings were scratched off or illegible from grime or water damage. Sometimes, Jacob felt he could almost read an entry, only to find the letters too blurred. He couldn't even read the headings. Scouring every inch of every page, he found nothing that could help him.

With a furious roar, he threw the menu down onto the tabletop, seriously fed up with whatever stupid game was going on here. Jacob was cold, starving, and completely done with this whole place.

A sudden rocking noise on the table startled him out of his heated thoughts. When he glanced around the table, he saw that another glass of water had replaced the half empty one. The ice clinking around in the glass seemed to taunt him, daring him to try to drink it again.

Then the shuffling sounded again, this time seeming as if it was coming from everywhere at once. Could it be an animal? Jacob shook his head, dismissing the thought immediately. He already knew there were no animals in here. He hadn't seen so much as a cockroach since he'd come in. Besides, that didn't explain how the water had gotten on his table, and how the other glass disappeared.

"Who's there?" he called out, kicking himself again for the fact that his voice rose in pitch and squeaked. "Whatever you're doing, it's not funny!"

The shuffling sounded again, seeming to move from table to table, faster and faster. Jacob ducked his head under the table again to make sure it wasn't an animal, but he couldn't see anything. He started to sweat again, the drops of perspiration leaving icy trails from his forehead, down his face, to his chin. Were there ghosts in this place? Maybe it was haunted. Jacob had never been one to believe in hauntings, but right now it seemed like the best explanation he had.

Something must have gone wrong when he'd called this place earlier. He'd misheard directions or something because this diner was not what was advertised on that phone message. This place was hideous, cold, and disgusting. There was something seriously wrong here, something...not normal happening. Had someone bought the place and changed the name recently? If that was the case, they'd run it into the ground. Maybe it had once been a nice place to eat, but now it was awful. Could the original owner be haunting the place, angry with the fact that his beloved diner was now in dirty shambles?

Jacob's racing thoughts were interrupted by what sounded like rattling dishes or glass breaking. He whipped his head towards the small order window, his heart beating so fast it sounded like a hum rather than individual beats. There hadn't been a peep from the kitchen until now, and that ominous feeling crept into the pit of his stomach again.

"Who's there?" he hollered again, his voice rising so high that he sounded like a choir boy rather than a grown man. He didn't care anymore about how his voice sounded, he just wanted to get out of here, get away from whatever was moving in the kitchen.

9

Another resounding crash sounded, making his heart race. Jacob looked, panicked, through the window. Everything was still whited out, to the point where he couldn't even see his car, though it was parked only a few feet away. When he looked back at the front door, he saw that the snow had blown up against the door in a drift six feet high. The storm, rather than easing up, was just getting worse.

A sudden, feral rage seemed to envelope Jacob. Jumping up from the booth seat, he snatched up the glass of water and hurled it against the wall, watching with a savage sort of satisfaction as it shattered into a million pieces. He felt sizzling droplets hit his skin from the explosion of the boiling water, but he didn't care.

"Somebody had better come out *right now*!" he snarled, all traces of the nervous squeak gone. His voice was low, guttural, enraged. "NOW!"

On some level, Jacob felt a little proud of himself for getting a little control over his fear. He stood tall, facing the kitchen, his hands fisted at his sides. Some of the adrenaline he'd felt when attacking the Jukebox returned, giving him a temporary boost of confidence.

A flicking sort of noise drew his attention back to the table where he'd been sitting. The hanging light over the table began to flicker on and off rapidly. Jacob stared at it in horrified fascination. The place didn't even seem to be wired properly, and he hadn't seen any kind of light from anywhere in the diner until now, excepting the light in the Jukebox. Then the light started to sway back and forth wildly, as if someone had pushed it with all their might. When the fixture finally stopped swaying, the light came on and didn't flicker anymore. The menu sat directly below the light, as if on a stage with a spotlight on it. Jacob got that feeling again, like something was going on unseen to him that he really didn't want to know about.

Slowly, Jacob approached the table, his brief flare of anger giving way once more to cold fear. As he approached the booth, he could see that the menu was now full of a tidy black script that looked as if it had been typed on an old typewriter. Jacob read the large, green letters at the top of the menu, his heart sinking.

The Despicable Diner

The menu now had the same lettering and logo as the glass did. So this place really was called *The Despicable Diner*. Picking up the menu with shaking hands, Jacob flipped through the pages of breakfast offerings, lunch specials, and dinner options. The last page had a full spread of desserts, all with pictures included.

As Jacob put the menu down, his head began to spin. Was he going back in time? Was this some sort of sick time loop? His heart, stretched to its limit already with the non-stop pounding, thudded hollowly in his chest. The sweat on his forehead formed an icy crust above his brow. The blizzard outside kept blowing snow against the door, almost as if the weather was purposely trying to trap him here.

Again, a sort of scratching noise sounded. Jacob turned towards it, his mouth dry, his heart constricted with dread. He wondered if the demonic Jukebox had resurrected itself and was now coming to finish him off. It was almost a relief when he saw that the abnormally tall sign that stood by the door had changed position. It now stood directly in front of his booth, no longer inviting diners to sit where they found a menu. Bold, black letters were inscribed across the white background, numbing Jacob from the head down as he read them.

ORDER NOW, OR ELSE.

Jacob's breathing became shallower. "Why...why do I have to order? There's nothing edible here."

Predictably, no answers came. Irritated, he stood up, moved the sign back to its place by the front door, then slouched back to the booth. He sat down, folding his arms across his torso, trying to catch his breath. A shudder rippled through his body as he rocked back and forth, once more wondering if he was going crazy. There was absolutely no way he was going to order. No, he had to get out of here. He had to bust out of the door, or just take his chances with the kitchen, or...

He glanced over at the window. It was huge, at least seven feet wide and five feet tall. The glass looked thick, and had likely grown inflexible with age, but he had to try something. Jacob looked around the room, trying to find something heavy enough to throw through the window. His hopes died as he looked around. There were no tables and chairs. The entire room was made up of booths along the wall and swiveling counter stools along the front counter that were bolted to the floor.

Jacob's gaze landed on the cash register. It was old and heavy. The more he thought about it, though, the more he realized that the heavy register hadn't budged at all when he'd pounded his fist on the counter. Either it was bolted down too, or it was stuck to the countertop with years of gooey grime.

There was only one answer. The Jukebox.

Before he could change his mind, Jacob bolted to his feet and raced through the archway to the room with the Jukebox. It still lay on its front, shattered into thousands of shards of glass. Finding a spot that wasn't riddled with glass, Jacob gripped the metal frame and tugged with all his might. He heaved the stupid thing around, trying to loosen the frame from the rest of the machine. No luck. It was attached firmly to the cabinet and record player.

Dropping the frame, Jacob cursed and kicked the Jukebox once more, than stomped back to the booth where he'd been sitting. With no other options, he snatched up the menu and sat down, searching each listing for any kind of clue. There had to be something on the menu now that he could read it. As he skimmed the breakfast pages, one entry caught his eye.

Pamcakes with Syrup

"Pamcakes?" he murmured to himself. Blinking hard, he peered down at the listing, his nose mere inches away from the page. Sure enough, it said *Pamcakes.*

"No...no, that can't be right. It's got to be wrong. Please be wrong. You have to be wrong!"

Jacob squinted at the menu, sure that it was just a typo. He had no idea why he was begging the menu to be wrong, but it just had to be. That was the only thing that made sense. As he continued reading, though, he realized that something really sick, really evil was going on here.

Pam made some great pancakes. Well, we made great pancakes. She just made for some good ingredients. The syrup is AB positive, very rare indeed, and delicious.

Jacob's mouth got, if possible, even more dry. AB negative? Was that some kind of horrible joke? AB positive was a blood type, one of the rarer types. And what did the menu mean that she made good ingredients? Were there *cannibals* working here? Could such a thing even really happen in this day and age?

His breathing grew shallow again, and he pushed the menu away from him as if it were a poisonous snake about to strike. When his heart rate slowed, he realized the connection between the license he'd found earlier in the drawer and the name on the menu. Why did that name sound so familiar? Jacob knew he'd seen that woman somewhere, had heard her name somewhere, but he just couldn't place it. What had happened to Pam?

Jacob gritted his teeth, a sense of determination rising inside him. He had to remember Pam, remember what happened to her. If he could...maybe he could try to find a way out of this mess. Whatever happened, he didn't want his fate to be the same as Pam's.

10

The answer came in a sudden flash. The woman's name was Pam Harkness. People up at Jacobs's school still talked about her. She'd been a student there a few years back. The police had found her car abandoned on the side of the highway, with no clues to where she had gone. It was as if she'd just parked, gotten out and vanished. No sign of a struggle. No accident. The car was perfectly intact.

Jacob had been riveted by the story, creating all sorts of possibilities in his mind. Everyone up at campus liked to talk about the story and speculate about how she'd gone missing. He'd imagined that she'd been picked up by an older couple who were secretly the leaders of a vast cult out in the country, or that she'd wandered off into the woods crying over lost love, only to fall into a river and drown. It had almost been like a game, trying to solve the unsolved disappearance.

The investigation, as far as he knew, was still ongoing. They'd never found her body, or any trace of her at all. Her parents and the police had put out a whole bunch of clues, saying that she was last seen heading to a party just a couple towns over, but had never shown up. She had taken a biology class in which she'd found out she had the rarest blood type, AB positive. The police had put that out there just in case they found her mangled remains or something and the blood type could help identify her.

But now it looked like he had solved it, and it wasn't so fun now that the same thing was happening to him. He swallowed hard. Had Pam been the one to push the SALE button on the cash register? Had she endured the screechy screaming from the Jukebox, too? Maybe she'd unplugged it in the first place. Maybe one of those plates of moldering food had been hers before she died.

Jacob stared down at the word "Pamcakes" on the menu, his dread growing. Had the diner really gotten her? Something must have happened to her here. Why else would her license be here? But if she'd come here and they'd never found her body, what had happened to her remains? And what exactly did it mean for Jacob? He tried to swallow and found he couldn't. He wished he could speak to Pam, even just for a few seconds to try to figure out what was going on.

Trying to keep his mind from his dark thoughts, Jacob picked up the menu again. Turning the pages of the menu with a strange, sick fascination, he scanned the dessert menu. Most of the offerings looked normal, like cakes, pies, ice cream. At least, they were normal, until he came to the milkshake.

Henry's Hearty Milkshake

Jacob's eyes moved slowly to the description beneath the heading. He didn't want to know what was in the hearty milkshake, but he just couldn't stop reading, almost as if some evil demon was holding his eyes open, forcing him to read.

Henry was always told that he had a big heart, and boy were they right. You'll need a knife and a straw for this frosty treat. You could dip your fingers into this despicable dessert, but you can have Henry's fingers to dip instead.

Jacob's mind raced. Henry...Henry...where had he heard that name? Just like Pam Harkness's name, it sounded familiar, though Henry was a little more common than Pam. But then Jacob realized that he'd heard the name Henry mentioned somewhere, but that the guy didn't go by Henry. Most people had called him by a nickname.

Yes, that was it. The strange story came slowly back to Jacob's mind, piece by piece, the memory a product of the hours he'd spent in of the television watching true crime stories. He'd seen something recently about a Hank Baskins, just a few weeks ago. And Hank was short for Henry.

The guy had worked for the city, in construction and roadworks, but he hadn't shown up for work one day. When he'd been missing for three days, they checked his apartment, only to find that he wasn't there. He'd simply vanished. He hadn't been seen since going home the day before work. Had the diner gotten him too?

Jacob's heart sank. The menu had held clues all right, but they were the kind of clues that only made him feel doomed, rather than helping him figure out what on earth was happening in this twisted place. His heart sank. Would he someday be another name on television, another random, unexplained disappearance?

The shuffling noises suddenly sounded again, even faster this time than they had been before, coming from everywhere at once. Jacob raised his arms reflexively in an attempt to protect himself. After the noises died down, Jacob turned towards the countertop and the kitchen beyond to see the sign from the front door standing right next to his booth again, shaking and creaking ominously as it swayed side to side.

Jacob let out an ear-splitting scream, borne of terror and rage, once more raising his hands over his head to protect himself. Before his very eyes, the sign's letters began to change again, some shuffling around and some erasing themselves as if they were an animated cartoon instead of words on a paper. Jacob stared at it, his mouth hanging open in dread.

ORDER NOW. LAST CHANCE.

"Order what?" he cried, holding the menu up in front of him like some sort of pathetic shield. "There's nothing that's even edible here!"

The sign stopped moving suddenly, the creaking and groaning noises stopping with it. Jacob's breaths came out in shuddering gasps. Slowly, the sign tilted towards him, not toppling over even though it was balanced only on the two front legs. The sight terri-fied Jacob so much that he screamed the first thing that came to mind. "HENRY'S HEARTY MILK-SHAKE!"

He shoved the menu away from him across the table, terrified to read anymore and discover any other missing person's cases. The minute he screamed the words, a terrible clatter sounded in the kitchen, as if people were fighting and breaking dishes in there. The lights began to flicker and sway overhead again. Jacob cowered in the booth, his hands over his head. Why was this happening to him? What was *wrong* with this place?

A crack like the sound of a gunshot sounded, and Jacob ducked below the table, covering his ears. He wondered if it was some kind of weapon or a bone snapping in half. Either scenario was equally horrifying. Smaller crackles sounded afterwards, al-most like joints creaking and cracking when a person stands up, but much louder. The sounds seemed to surround him as he pushed himself as flat against the wall as he could get.

All of the lights went out suddenly, plunging the diner into darkness. Footsteps sounded in the dark-ness, raising Jacob's terror to an all-time high. His breaths came in sobbing, shuddering, unnatural sounds as a shadowy figure emerged from behind the counter at the front of the diner. It was vaguely humanoid. Jacob could make out long, gangly legs and arms, an impossibly thin torso, and a large head in the dim light from the window. Jacob noticed that the thing had to crouch as it came through the archway to the far left of the counter, even though it was at least seven feet tall.

It's a monster, Jacob realized with growing dread. *This must be the thing that's going to end my life.*

Jacob pushed himself even harder against the wall next to the booth, trying to get as far away from the thing as possible. It crept closer, that creaking, cracking noise sounding with every slow step as it made its way slowly to Jacob's booth. Jacob's heart was racing so hard he felt sure it would slam through his rib cage at any moment. That, or he would die of a prolonged, elevated heart rate.

The thing was pencil thin, and as it came closer, Jacob saw that it was wearing a purple and green sailor shirt with a matching hat, like it was some horrible parody of Popeye. The thing's head was so round and wide that Jacob wondered how it didn't topple right off of the creature's thin frame. Its eyes were sunken and white, with no irises or pupils. They had a soulless quality about them that made Jacob's hair stand on end.

As the thing stopped right next to the table, it extended its arm, holding out a tall, frosty glass of ice cream, topped with a cherry and...a beating, human heart. Jacob screamed again, seeing black at the edges of his vision. Was this how he would die? Passing out before this creature, only for it to cut out his heart for the next milkshake?

11

The creature leered at Jacob, holding up a can of whipped cream with the other hand, ready to add it to the dessert. Jacob started to dry heave, but he wasn't sure if the reaction came from the actual human heart on the milkshake, or the creature itself. Maybe both.

Oddly, the creature turned and sat in a different booth, still clutching the milkshake and the whipped cream. It set the cup and the can down on the table, then looked at Jacob with those terrible eyes. It raised one long, bony finger, and pointed at the seat across from it. The message was clear. He wanted Jacob to sit at the table with him.

Jacob hesitated only a second, not wanting to make the thing mad. If he made that monster angry, Jacob could bet that it would be the last thing he'd ever do.

With anxious, shuffling steps, he got up and moved across the diner to the seat. He scooted into the booth, suddenly suppressing a hysterical laugh. The whole ordeal felt like some horrific blind date gone wrong. He knew that people sometimes laughed at inappropriate times, like at funerals, but now he understood why.

The minute he settled into the seat, leaning back as far away from the thing as he could, the creature scooted the milkshake across the table to him, staring at him with those white, unblinking eyes. Jacob cringed away from it, not even daring to rest his hands on the same table as that abomination. The creature leaned forward, cocking its head as if studying Jacob. Finally, it spoke, its voice strangely chipper, a stark contrast from its awful appearance.

"Do you know why you're here?"

Jacob stared at him, his mouth agape. The voice sounded oddly familiar. Where had he heard it before? He forgot his panic for a few moments when he remembered.

"Your voice...I recognize it. You're the one from the phone message telling me to come here. You *tricked* me!"

In a sudden fit of bravery, Jacob pointed an accusing finger at the thing. The creature shook its head, the creaking, groaning noise sounding as it did so. It leaned its elbows on the table, clasping its hands with the unnaturally long fingers in front of it. "Jacob, nobody tricked you. You called me, remember?"

"No I didn't," Jacob responded, his voice rising with hysteria. "The ad in the yellow pages, the message machine, it was all a trick! You said there was food here, but there wasn't! You lied!"

The creature shook its head again and made a little tsk-tsking noise. "You see, Jacob, playing dumb is exactly how you end up on our menu. So tell the truth. Why are you here?"

Jacob was shaking so badly now that his teeth were rattling, but he couldn't quite ignore the surge of defiance that rose up inside him. "I...I was just hungry, that's all! I was told you had food here, I followed the directions and it brought me here!"

A smile split the creature's face, revealing a row of too-large teeth that sent horrible shivers down Jacob's spine. "Sure, Jacob. You were just hungry. You're just the victim here, aren't you?"

Jacob's breaths came in small pants, making him sound almost like a dog. "I'm not saying I'm a victim, I'm saying I was told a lie and tricked into coming here!"

The creature put its arms down flat on the table and shook its overlarge head. "Everyone who comes to *The Despicable Diner* comes for a very specific reason, Jacob. Tell me why you have that limp."

Jacob stared at the thing, openmouthed. "Why do you want to know about that? That doesn't have anything to do with you or this place!"

The creature's grin grew wider. "Just tell me."

Still not wanting to anger the thing, Jacob gave a timid shrug. "I just played a stupid prank on a friend. That's all it was. It-it was just a prank and...and also an accident. It was a prank that ended up as an accident. What do you know about it?"

The thing raised one bony finger and tilted it back and forth. "Jacob, you're going to have to tell me more than that. You're going to have to be specific. It's important for me to know all the details."

Jacob gulped, then wound up in a fit of coughing as his dry throat rebelled. The creature just stared at him, waiting for the coughing to subside. He gave a nervous shrug, avoiding the creature's awful white eyes. "We were roommates at Iowa State. I thought it'd be funny if I jumped out and scared him on the back deck of our apartment with a Halloween mask. It was just a stupid idea, I didn't mean for..."

Jacob trailed off hopelessly, his face contorting as he relived the awful scene. The creature lifted its hands, leaning its elbows on the table and steepling its fingers. "Mm hmm. And then what happened?"

Tears began to trickle out of Jacob's eyes. "He...he was scared so he grabbed me. I started to lose my balance, so I tried to fight him off, and we both fell over the edge of the balcony. I broke a few bones in my leg when I landed on him...and he...he didn't m-make it."

It felt as if the story had been wrenched from him. He'd never told this story to anyone, instead telling his other roommates, the other kids on his floor, the campus administration, even his parents that his friend had died of a skull fracture, not from anything Jacob had done. The kid's family hadn't pressed charges, and everything seemed to work out okay, but knowing the truth had always haunted Jacob since that horrible night.

"That's right, Jacob. That's right." The creature's smile only grew bigger as Jacob kept the confession moving forward. "He died because of you."

"It was an accident," Jacob replied sharply. "Just a stupid accident. I would never have done anything like that on purpose. He was my best friend, my only friend! And I lost him! Then everyone else didn't want anything to do with me because of what happened. I had to drop out, and my parents don't know. I just can't go back!"

The tears came pouring out fresh as Jacob relived the horror of seeing his friend lying there, motionless, hurt, becoming a ghost right before Jacob's eyes. The memory twisted up his insides, making him start to feel ill again.

The thing's expression grew skeptical rather than sympathetic. It's smile hardened, taking on a sinister quality that made Jacob shrink away from it. "Okay, sure, Jacob. This all must be so hard for you. Never mind your friend who died because of you."

A keening sort of wail rose out of Jacob. The creature was voicing all the thoughts that had plagued Jacob for over a year now.

The creature's grin grew wide once more. "And what happened after that, Jacob?"

Jacob paused, trying to get his shuddering, panicking mind to remember. He thought back to the days after the initial investigation, but he seemed to come up against a large, blank wall. "I...I don't remember, actually. I don't remember a funeral, or the police getting involved or...I don't know. Nothing happened, it just sort of...went away."

The creature leaned forward, that leering smile still in place. "Look at the menu, see if anything looks familiar."

Though he didn't want to, Jacob looked down at the open page of the menu just one last time. There was only one entry on the whole page now, in big, black, bold letters. Jacob's tears began to flow again as he looked at the words.

"WALKER'S CHICKEN AND WAFFLES." Jacob's voice cracked on the last word as he read the sentence. Walker, the last name of his old roommate and friend. More tears walled up in Jacob's eyes, and the creature's permanent smile grew even bigger.

"I want you to order it, Jacob."

"NO!" Jacob hollered, his voice breaking once again from the emotion. "I won't! You can't make me!"

The creature's smile took on a menacing air. "Order it, or you're going to be next on the menu."

12

Though it felt like years had passed since the conversation with the terrifying creature began, it had really only been a few minutes. Jacob had sat tall and rigid in the booth when he'd first confronted the creature, but now he sagged against the seat, his tears coming in fits and starts. Having some horrible thing tell him how awful he was, when he'd already spent the last eighteen months of his life telling himself that very same thing, was the worst torture he could have imagined. He almost wished that he'd been haunted by a or poltergeist. It would be so much easier than this.

As Jacob sobbed brokenly in the booth, the creature sitting across from him, its horrible smile still in place, Jacob began to understand something. The Despicable Diner wasn't the name of the building at all. It was the name of the creature. This thing...whatever it was, lured people here, preyed on their insecurities, their fears, their regrets, their past mistakes, then used those ingredients to cook up truly horrible meals. Judging by the creature's thinness, it was never satisfied, and had to keep luring people here to satisfy its hunger...for what? Broken hearts? Regret? Feelings of self-loathing?

The creepy, dilapidated building was the creature's domain, separate from the outside world, a place where it could perform its horrors. Jacob's stomach clenched at the thought. All his silly escape ideas, the plan to wait out the storm, the doomed thoughts about smashing the window or escaping out the back door of the kitchen...he knew now that they were all foolish, idiotic thoughts. There was no escape. He should have listened to that gut instinct and stayed outside the diner while he still had the chance. The moment he'd opened the door and stepped inside, he'd sealed his fate.

The rest of his life, as it was, would be today only, however long the Diner allowed that to be. The realization brought on a fresh wave of tears. He thought once more about the fact that he was totally alone. How long would it take for anyone to notice Jacob was missing? As a rule, he avoided people. The guilt from Walker's death had made him even less social than he'd already been.

He hadn't lived with any roommates. He hadn't even been to school in over a year, having lost his enrollment status. He'd never even had a job here in Iowa, so there was no angry boss to go calling around for him when he didn't show up to work. The only person who would eventually notice that he was gone was his landlord when the rent came due. That, or his parents when he didn't pick up his mother's calls.

His stomach clenched at the thought of his mom and dad. Would he be the lead story at some point on the true crime mysteries he liked to watch so much? Would they see him on the news or on one of those shows and spend the rest of their lives wondering what had happened to him?

The creature seemed happy to wait through Jacob's despair, smiling and staring at him with those blank eyes. The thing never blinked, not even once, a fact that Jacob found increasingly unnerving. Jacob parted his cracked, dry lips and took a shuddering breath. He had an idea. It wasn't much of a chance, but he had to take it.

"Can I take the milkshake to go?" he finally asked, finding the nerve to look back up at the Diner. It was a sad joke, Jacob knew, but humor had always been his fallback during stressful times. He'd joked casually about Walker anytime it came up until people grew disgusted with him. He knew it hadn't been right to joke around about Walker's bad habits of leaving dirty underwear around, but it was the only coping mechanism he had. He didn't do it disrespectfully. He just wasn't sure how else to manage.

He'd always been okay at talking his way out of things. His mother had dealt with him wiggling out of everything from school to baseball practice. Maybe it could work here. Besides, if Jacob was going to die here, he wanted to at least have the last laugh.

It looked like the creature had other plans, though. An ominous chuckle, like the sound of grinding metal, came out of its mouth. The creature's grin stretched wider, its teeth looking as if they were taking over its whole face. The laugh took Jacob aback. He hadn't expected it to laugh, or even have a sense of humor at all. He could sense the waves of evil coming off of it, so hearing it laugh only unnerved Jacob more.

"That's a good one, Jacob," it said in that high-pitched, creepily cheerful voice. "But no, you can't leave until you order. And you have to finish your plate. Those are the rules."

Jacob looked dubiously at the milkshake, wrinkling his nose when the heart actually *twitched*. He felt bile rising in his throat again and pushed it away.

"I can't," he said. "Not with...not with that heart in it."

The Diner's eyes went wide. "Oh, no, I don't want you to eat the milkshake. That would be far too easy."

The hairs on the back of Jacob's neck prickled. "What do you mean, too easy?"

The creature gestured once more towards the menu, where the words "WALKERS CHICKEN AND WAFFLES" had gotten bigger and bolder. The text seemed to stare at Jacob, mocking him, reminding him of the worst mistake he'd ever made, all for the sake of a laugh. Mustering up every last ounce of courage he had, Jacob shook his head.

"I don't want to order that. And I'm not eating anything from this forsaken place."

The hunger he'd felt so forcefully before had dulled, no longer even registering with him anymore. Jacob didn't want to eat ever again. He didn't deserve to eat, or to breathe, or see his family, or ever enjoy *anything* anymore. The creature across from him seemed to swell, that awful, grinding chuckle sounding once again.

The Diner was enjoying it. He wanted Jacob to feel terrible. The longer Jacob sat there, the more he realized that the creature must be feeding off of his emotions, his terror, his guilt. Putting an item on the menu with Walker's name on it, and trying to force him to order it, was producing all these feelings. The creature seemed to laugh mockingly at him any time he felt a surge of remorse, so that must be the explanation.

"You have to order it, Jacob. Snacking on bits of your so-called best friend can't be any worse than killing him, now, can it?" The creature cocked it's head, its blank eyes somehow challenging and taunting Jacob at the same time.

Jacob had never realized it before, but ever since Walker's death, he'd only eaten out of absolute necessity when he couldn't ignore his hunger any longer. It wasn't fair that he was alive, and Walker wasn't. Maybe getting trapped in this diner was exactly what he deserved. He knew without a doubt that the Diner wasn't going to show any mercy, so he had to go down with honor, like a captain sinking with the ship. Leveling his gaze on the creature, he felt a sudden clarity of mind.

"I'm not ordering my best friend. You can make me into a meatloaf or scrambled eggs or whatever you're going to do, but I'm not eating my friend."

Jacob felt a sudden surge of pride as he sat up tall, staring the creature down. His voice didn't waver. He felt a strong determination to not fail Walker again, to not chicken out as he'd done before. If these truly were his last moments, he wanted to use them to honor Walker's life, rather than trying to save his own.

The creature tsk-tsked again, his weird voice taking on a menacing note of warning. "Last chance, Jacob. You can do what needs to be done and I'll make you forget everything that happened. Wouldn't you like that? To be able to forget all of this and just...walk away?"

Jacob paused, surprisingly tempted by the offer. He could forget about Walker? Leave this horrible place, go back to his apartment, try to salvage something of his life? He couldn't deny that the offer was appealing. Jacob's eyes moved back down to the menu as a cold sweat broke out on his brow again.

13

The more he thought about it, the more Jacob couldn't imagine this horrible thing across from him showing any mercy. Would the creature really let him forget about Walker? Was it really as simple as eating some horrible menu offering involving his dead friend? Jacob swallowed hard as he gazed around the diner, with its empty, cobwebby tables, dingy, flickering lights, and desolate air.

No, the creature wouldn't just give him such an easy out. Yes, it was disgusting to eat something that may or may not have bits of his friend in it, but it still seemed too simple, too painless. Anyone who came to this diner never made it out, that much was clear. And did he really want to take such a cowardly path again? Even if it was true, it was a horrible offence to Walker's memory. Jacob knew he would never do it.

Looking back at the Diner, Jacob shook his head, his hands tightening into fists. "I don't trust you. You feed off of people's emotions. You like it when people are hurt and distressed and remorseful. You want to feed off more of that, and I'm not giving that to you."

The creature's mouth opened in a large, exaggerated *O*. "You don't mean that, surely, Jacob. Come on, now. Just one meal, and all your troubles are gone. You'll find yourself back at your grubby little apartment with no memory of what you did to poor Walker. You won't even be hungry anymore until it's time to eat again. You'll feel nice and warm, too. Doesn't that sound nice?"

Jacob tried to inject as much insult into his next words as possible. "Those empty tables and that rotted food tell me that nobody ever got past the first few bites. You're just lying to get what you want. The answer is no. Don't ask me about it again."

The creature gave a little chuckle that ended in a sigh. "Just as well, Jacob. You're right. I *was* lying. Such a shame, it's so much more fun when my food gives in to temptation. Makes my next meal so much tastier. Ah, well. You win some, you lose some."

Jacob's face grew red. "In my case, and everyone else who's come into this horrible place, we all lose! You're a *monster* for doing what you do!"

The creature stood up, its joints creaking and cracking as it moved its warped body. "Of course I'm a monster. What did you expect?"

It took a few steps, then turned back towards Jacob, that awful smile still in place, its eyes still blank and soulless. "Before I make your food, I've got a little something I want you to see. I'll be back soon to see how you liked my little film."

With a dark chuckle, the creature ambled back to the kitchen, creaking and cracking as it went. Jacob stared at the milkshake, disgusted, wishing the creature hadn't left it there. The ice cream or whatever it was had started to melt, the purplish substance running down the sides of the cup.

A sudden sound blared from the opposite side of the diner, an upbeat anthem played, sounding like the type of music that would play at the start of a sports game or a play. A large, white rectangle appeared on the opposite wall, which eventually started playing a picture, as if there were a video projector behind him. The movie, or whatever it was, started outside the diner.

Jacob sat staring in horrified fascination as the Despicable Diner appeared on the screen, waving a cheery greeting as if he were filming some sort of weird training video instead of describing the horrors of eating people. The cheery music continued, making Jacob feel sick to his stomach.

"Hello!" said the Diner. "Welcome to the Despicable Diner. Before we talk about making food, let's take a look around the old place, shall we? Just bought the place and I must say, I'm thrilled to finally have a place to make my...meals."

The diner in the background of the video looked completely different than the diner of here and now, likely looking as the diner would have done in its prime. The booths and countertops were sparkling and clean, with a beautiful white and red finish, rather than the dingy gray all around Jacob. The cash register sat on the counter, painted in a cheerful red and polished to a mirror shine. Jacob had thought it was brown. As the camera panned over to the Jukebox, Jacob noticed that it was playing some kind of 50s doo-wop song, its exterior clean and new rather than warped and yellowed with age.

When he looked at the floors in the movie, Jacob saw that they were tiled in black and white, a stark contrast to the solid black they were now. The thought made him shudder as he wondered how many years of dirt and grime he'd been walking on. He shuddered even more as he wondered how many people had been lost to this awful thing over the years. Now he hoped that all those people he'd imagined before he came into the diner hadn't actually been sucked into this trap. Jacob wished desperately that he could post some kind of warning to people.

"Isn't this place swell?" the creature continued. "Folks come from all over to enjoy the music, make some friends, and lose their souls for their past crimes. Sort of gives a new meaning to the phrase 'justice is served,' doesn't it?"

The creature in the video chuckled as if eating people was the most hilarious thing in the world. Jacob's heart sank. Clearly, there had been many, many more victims before him. The thought made him choke up. Jacob cringed away from the creature's cheery tone and smile, wanting to look away, but finding that he couldn't.

Another wave of despair crashed over him as he thought about how stupid he'd been to go inside the diner, to let his hunger get to the point of desperation, to forget to go grocery shopping. He'd never see his family again. He'd never go to another movie, or spend another day getting lost in the mall. He'd never have another chance to try to make friends. It was all over. His life was over.

"Let me take you on back to the kitchen," the creature said in the video. Jacob's heart began to throb as the camera followed the monster behind the counter. The space behind the front counter was immaculate in the video, completely clear of all the debris that Jacob had had to climb around. The creature took Jacob's same path around the corner to the kitchen door.

As the thing approached the kitchen door, Jacob felt a thrill of horror, but the inside of the kitchen looked like any ordinary restaurant kitchen. Chrome dishwashers and fridges stood at odd intervals around the room, complemented here and there by gleaming countertops and stovetops. A large grill stood at the opposite end of the room, free of grease and grime, looking as if it had just been installed.

"We start by collecting a little memento from our guests, something for others to remember them by.

It could be ID, or a treasured piece of jewelry, or even some clothing!"

Jacob's mind flashed to the cash register. That was why it didn't even have any money. It was filled with items taken from the other poor folks who'd accidentally wandered into the diner and never been seen again. Sweat poured down Jacob's face as he wondered what the creature would take from him and put into the cash register. It would just become another memento of a poor, lost soul.

The camera in the movie switched back suddenly to the cash register. The drawer was open, the same strange mixture of knick-knacks and other things lining the inside. In the video, the camera cut back to the kitchen, where the creature grinned.

"Once our new food source has been put to sleep, they're taken here to the kitchen."

The creature indicated a large machine that looked like a giant dough mixer of some sort. "This is our grinder and separator. If we're making pie or soup or tacos with our new friend, this is the best machine to use to separate that lovely, meaty muscle from those pesky bones."

He gave another lighthearted laugh, and Jacob realized with a growing sense of dread that the machine was big enough for a full-grown man. The creature stepped over to another part of the kitchen, where a massive oven stood alongside one wall.

"This is our deluxe, super-size oven. We use the oven if we're planning on making roast or fried food out of our guests. This state-of-the-art technology gets that flesh roasted to just the right amount of juiciness. So *tasty*!"

14

The Diner then led the camera to the biggest cutting board Jacob had ever seen. Above the board, several wicked looking kitchen knives hung on the wall, including serrated knives and a large meat cleaver. They were far larger than ordinary kitchen knives, clearly intended to butcher larger cuts of meat. Jacob tried to swallow, but his dry throat only constricted more tightly.

"Our top-of-the-line knives and cutting surface make it possible to cut and fry fingers from up to five patrons at once! We know how finger-licking good our guilt-ridden guests can be, so we try to keep up production as much as possible."

He gave another cheery laugh, the sound grating on Jacob's nerves. He wondered wildly if there were more creatures like the Despicable Diner. Did they all feast on human flesh like this crazed maniac? Was this some kind of hub for monsters of all descriptions to come and feast on the flesh of human beings? Had whole groups of people accidentally wound up here and been eaten by some crazed group of flesh-eating monsters? The thought sickened him as he sagged against the back of the booth.

As all these terrible realizations began to take hold, Jacob started to hyperventilate. He wanted to do the right thing by having the courage to face the creature, but hadn't he already proven his courage by not falling for the Diner's lie? He'd refused to eat any remnants of his best friend, whether they were real or not. So did that mean he could try to run? Or did that still make him a coward?

The more he thought about being chopped up on that table, or ground in that machine, the more Jacob knew he had to survive. If anything, he had to find a way to warn others away from the diner, to keep this from happening again. Wouldn't that be the more courageous thing to do? The desire to get free and help other potential victims gave him a much-needed surge of energy. He felt a sudden, anxious urge to get out of here, to do *anything* it took to survive.

As the camera angle in the video changed once again, Jacob found that he couldn't resist watching for just a little longer. Maybe if he acted like he was doing what the creature wanted, he could buy some time to devise an escape plan. Yes, that was the right thing to do. Plan and calculate carefully instead of just trying to barge his way out.

In the movie, the Diner now stood at the gleaming stove, holding the handle of a pan as he fried something up. He wore a white apron with the diner logo and the words *The Despicable Diner* splashed across it in the same green and purple text. Lifting the pan, he tossed the contents up, and Jacob's stomach lurched. The contents of the pan looked suspiciously like human fingers. The monster turned to face the camera, that awful, permanent grin stretched across his face. The creature put the pan back on the stove and took a deep breath in.

"Smells like the fingers are ready! Let's put them on the sideboard to let the grease drain off."

The creature busied himself putting the fried fingers or whatever they were on a paper-towel lined plate. As he finished, the camera panned over to a large shelf above the stove. Gesturing to some bottles on a shelf above the pans, the creature splayed out his hands like a game show host showing off some coveted prizes.

"Check out our in-house line of spices and flavorings, taken directly from our patrons! Guilt and remorse are sprinkled into every dish, but you can also try fear for a spicier flavor! Why not use Screams of the Damned for a little extra kick? Or for a smoother, sweeter flavor, try desperation and regret! You'll love the taste of your coffee with the tears of our hopeless victims."

Jacob's heart began to race. Would he wind up as someone's grilled cheese sandwich and fries? What if the Diner ground his bones into powder and sprinkled it over some kind of demonic soup? Would he wind up as a breakfast item? Some kind of steak? A pizza with all his body parts used as toppings? The thought made him force down yet another wave of nausea.

Once again, he fought desperately to find an escape, any escape. Should he try to bolt across the room to the front door? If he was desperate enough, he might be able to get outside. Maybe with enough force, he could push against the pile of snow.

"Today," the video continued, "we're making human pot pie. For this delectable dish, we'll need one wretched soul, roasted at 500 degrees for thirty minutes exactly."

Despite Jacob's fear, he found his eyes moving back to the video. It was like looking at the aftermath of some horrible car crash or train accident. He really didn't want to look at it, but found he couldn't help it.

"Next, we make our gravy. Be sure to mix in plenty of remorse, along with a hefty helping of unbearable sadness, which gives the gravy its signature smoothness. Just look at that steamy goodness!"

The camera panned to an enormous pie pan filled halfway with a light brown gravy and overlarge potatoes and carrots. In the middle, there was a disturbingly human shaped lump. Jacob tore his eyes away from the screen, gagging with every breath. The horror of it all had finally become too much.

The video droned on behind him, but he knew he couldn't look back at it. With every last ounce of fight he still had, he dragged himself out of the booth and staggered to the door. He stumbled the last few steps and grabbed desperately for the door handle, the top of the handle slicing into his palm as he used it to bring himself upright again.

With an angry roar, he pushed on the door with all his might. It didn't budge. With a deep breath, he stepped back, then rammed the door as hard as possible. It still didn't budge. Frantic, Jacob rammed against the door again and again, stopping only when he realized that his shoulder hurt terribly. From somewhere behind him, he heard maniacal laughter.

"Yes, Jacob, keep trying to escape! Desperation is oh so flavorful for dishes. Keep trying! Maybe you'll get it eventually!"

The creature's taunts only made Jacob angrier. Heaving with all his might, he slammed against the door again, but it didn't budge even an inch. More tears of utter hopelessness poured down his cheeks as he banged his fist uselessly against the door.

After several minutes of fruitless tries, Jacob ran to the window and pounded against it. His injured hand screamed with every hit, but he didn't care. All he wanted was to get out of there, get away from that horrible thing. Even though his whole existence felt meaningless, he still didn't want to go this way.

He could turn things around. He could be a better person. He *would* be a better person if he managed to get out of here.

The thick, warped glass didn't even crack under Jacob's blows. He backed away, his chest heaving, his brow and lower back once more drenched in sweat. There had to be a way. There was always a way.

Looking behind him, he remembered the door leading to the kitchen, and the door beyond which might lead him out of here. It was a slim chance, but it was his only chance. Turning towards the kitchen, he bolted for the space behind the counter, ignoring the throbbing in his shoulder and hand.

He rounded the edge of the counter, vaulting over the crates of broken bottles, the cracked eggs, the trash everywhere. Jacob made it as far as the cash register when that horrible, cheerful voice said, "Oh, no, you don't!"

15

Jacob felt himself being pulled back, as if he was being sucked into some kind of giant vacuum. The force yanked him back to the booth where he'd been sitting. Jacob scrambled for purchase, trying to hold onto the edge of the counter or the seat of another booth. He even swung his hands wildly towards the too-tall sign, with no luck.

When his backside slammed down into the seat of the booth, he found he could no longer move, as if the force was now pinning him to the seat. He struggled and writhed as the creature approached once more. The thing shook his finger as he took the seat opposite Jacob, tsk tsking as if Jacob had been a naughty child running away from his mother.

"Now, Jacob, that was very rude! You didn't even tell me how you liked the video," the Diner said, tilting his head to the side. "I don't think you even finished watching it. It's really bad manners to walk out in the middle of a movie, you know. But if you really want to skip to step one of the cooking process, we can."

Moving one long, bony arm towards Jacob, the creature reached out. Jacob writhed away from it, trying desperately not to let it touch him. The monster plucked the forgotten twenty-dollar bill out of the front pocket of Jacob's shirt. The thing's grin grew wider. "Look at that! Some money. This will make a nice little addition to our collection of last items. Should confuse the next poor soul to make their way here, too."

The monster chuckled as he examined the torn, crumpled bill. With the same long, bony arm, he reached out towards the cash register, pushed the sale button, and stowed the twenty away with the other lost items. Jacob's heart began to thud so loudly he thought for sure it would break ribs. He had to get out! He *had* to! That one desperate refrain pounded through his frenzied mind over and over and over again.

Gritting his teeth, Jacob tried once more to move, but he could only move his head side to side. His arms were frozen to his sides, his legs glued together, his bottom firmly stuck to the booth. A guttural roar of pain and sheer terror rose up out of him, coming from depths in his soul he didn't even know he had.

"You can't do this to people!" Jacob screamed, fear and adrenaline making his voice sound almost feral. "You *can't*!"

The creature just grinned that horrible grin and tapped the tips of his fingers together. "That may be, but the things you did are just as despicable, Jacob. You tell me you don't remember a funeral, or talking to the police, but it all happened. You're just such a selfish jerk that you blocked it all out. You didn't even bother to attend the funeral. That's how horrible you are. So it's only fair that we take those horrible qualities and turn them into something tasty, isn't it?"

"No!" Jacob sobbed. "No! It was a mistake, the worst one I've ever made, but people can change! I felt like I couldn't go to the funeral. His family probably hates me!"

The creature shook its overlarge head. "But you lied, Jacob. You lied to his family, to the police. They all thought it was just a tragic accident, but you never told them that scaring him was your idea. You never told them that you only survived because his body broke your fall. You're a despicable human being, Jacob. Only truly despicable people make their way here. It happens to all horrible people eventually. You've done awful things, Jacob, and you deserve to *suffer*."

Another desperate scream wrenched from Jacob as he tried to move again. The creature nodded its head slowly. "Yes, you're horrible, Jacob. Drown in that guilt. Give in to it!"

"I'm NOT horrible!" Jacob sobbed. "It was a mistake! People make mistakes all the time!"

The creature began to nod, slowly up and down. "Oh, yes, you are horrible. People make mistakes, yes, but only good people don't try to cover them up. Goodbye, Jacob."

"No!" Jacob screamed, but the creature wasn't listening.

The grotesque head nodded faster, faster, faster, so fast that it became a blur. Amid the fear and panic blasting its way through Jacob's body, he wondered what was going on with the thing, why it was nodding its head so fast. The light fixtures flickered and began to sway as if in a high wind. Jacob hadn't seen all the lights on at once in the diner before, but the effect was somehow more terrifying than the awful dimness from before.

Looking back at the creature, Jacob watched with a sick sort of fascination as the thing's body began to rock back and forth. The motion shook the table, which then began to rattle all the tables in the diner, making the place look like it was experiencing a massive earthquake. The disgusting milkshake, the heart still twitching at random intervals, spilled over, dumping ice cream and the heart all over the table. Jacob cringed away, feeling nausea rise in his stomach as the milkshake splattered all over him. His screams of protest became sobs, endless, racking sobs that shook his whole body.

The lights flickered more quickly now, almost strobing in the speed of the flickering. Jacob's head felt ready to split open from pain. Between the shaking room, the vibrating Diner, the rattling tables, and the swaying light fixtures, it all became too much. A horrible, screeching laugh came from the creature as it continued to sway, faster and faster.

"We've only just begun, Jacob! This is what happens to despicable people!"

Jacob only moaned in response. He jumped suddenly as a loud crackling noise sounded overhead. Jacob realized to his horror that the lightbulb in the fixture had shattered. From the fixture came a sort of bolt of lightning, shooting down and scorching the disgusting tablecloth that covered the table. The heat from the scorch mark burned a large circle in the tablecloth. The acrid smell of burning plastic invaded Jacob's nostrils, making his stomach heave once more.

His vision began to fade and blur, and he realized he was going in and out of consciousness. Jacob wasn't sure whether it was the sizzling tablecloth, the burst lightbulb, or the creature's sick smile that made him want to end it all. Most likely, it was all of those things, combined with his splitting headache.

As he gazed stupidly around the room, the floor seemed to stretch out wide like a mouth yawning open, ready to devour him whole. The booths became abnormally tall, stretching up towards the ceiling. And the creature...it was nothing more than a purplish, greenish blur, still buzzing around like a hyped-up squirrel on caffeine. Everything wobbled and stretched, making Jacob wonder if his vision was starting to suffer from the ordeal.

Leaning back against the cracked, plasticky seat, Jacob closed his eyes, the swaying and stretching making him feel sick again. It was all too much. At this point, he was praying desperately for the end, anything but this madness. He just wanted to fall asleep and never wake up.

And suddenly, it all stopped. Jacob opened his eyes. The light fixtures, the tables, the floor, even the Diner was back to normal, or as normal as anything in this crazy place could be. The ringing silence made Jacob's head hurt even more. He blinked a few times, wondering if it had all been a bad dream. His breathing was shallow, his pulse weak. Maybe he'd passed out in the booth. A surge of hope filled him, until he looked across the table and saw the creature still sitting there. He'd stopped shaking, but the tablecloth was still scorched and covered in spilled ice cream.

The creature grinned evilly, leaning towards Jacob across the table. Too tired and ill to protest, Jacob didn't even try to move away. He knew in his heart that this was the end. In a way, it was sort of a relief.

"And now, Jacob, you're ready."

Reaching out, the creature's long, bony fingers twined their way twice around Jacob's thin palm.

Jacob had no energy to try to pull away or resist. His hand hung limply in the creature's bony fingers. The edges of Jacob's vision blackened. The last thing he saw was the creature rising out of his seat, leaning across the table towards Jacob. Its face came closer, staring at him again, mere inches away from his face, that horrible smile still in place.

16

One Month Later...

"Hello?"

Terry stood panting, having wrenched open the door to get into the old diner. She looked around the room, bewildered. It seemed to be some kind of old timey diner. The place looked as if it had been deserted for decades now, a thick layer of cobwebs and grime everywhere. She'd seen the dirt road off to the side of I-35 and turned off, hoping to shelter from the sudden freak storm in the small building she'd seen in the distance. Out here, there weren't too many places to shelter in the event of a sudden storm. Even though the place gave her the creeps, it had to be better than running out the gas in her car and freezing to death.

As she stepped inside, though, Terry noticed that the place wasn't much warmer on the inside. In fact, it almost felt colder. The building probably didn't have any working heating or cooling anymore. Terry rubbed her hands along her arms, trying desperately to warm up. If this place was colder than the outside, then there was no point sheltering here.

"Hello?" she called again, an edge of anxiety in her voice. Someone had to be here, surely. Abandoned places were almost always stripped of everything they had, and a place this old would have had almost everything taken by looters. At the very least, the place should be crawling with wild animals, but she didn't see any, so that meant that someone had to be kind of maintaining the place...right?

She looked back at the door, then into the diner again, wondering whether she should leave or stay. She'd made up her mind to turn around and go when she noticed a sign. Terry hadn't seen it at first because it was so freakishly tall that she had to tilt her head back to read it.

One simple sentence was printed in black letters on the white background; ***Seat Yourself Where You Find a Menu.***

Terry raised her eyebrows. That was odd. She'd never been to any place with such a weird sign, or a place where you could only sit where there was a menu. With a shrug, she clutched the strap of her purse more tightly and looked around the tables. Only one table had a menu on it, the booth closest to an ancient, crusty looking counter with a decrepit old cash register on it. An odd, purple stain was spread across the tablecloth, and a huge burn mark spread across the middle. Surely a candle wouldn't have done that. The thought made the hairs on the back of her rise.

Terry's nerves began to jangle the longer she stood there, wondering if she should sit. Why hadn't the city knocked this place down? It was absolutely filthy, every surface covered in at least a half inch of dust. She caught sight of cartons and plates of old food covered in moldy green fuzz on the countertop, along with crates of broken bottles on the floor behind the counter and moldy fruit. And yet, the place didn't stink like it probably should have.

There was something very wrong about this place. How long had it been abandoned? Terry turned again to leave, opting to keep driving in the storm until she found a gas station or someone's house, anywhere but here to wait out the storm. As she got to the door and pushed, though, it wouldn't budge. A ton of snow had already piled up against the door in just a matter of minutes.

"Seriously?" she muttered to herself. "That's not even possible. It wasn't even snowing that hard just a few minutes ago."

When she turned back around to face the diner, the weirdly tall sign was right behind her, almost as if someone had moved it. She jumped back, her heart thudding in her chest, wondering once again what on earth was wrong with this place. When her heart rate finally slowed, she noticed that the writing had changed. The nice cursive from before was gone, replaced by angry looking all caps. "ORDER NOW, OR ELSE."

Terry scurried away from the sign, moving further into the dining room, the hairs on the back of her neck standing on end. Her heart pounded wildly in her ears, her throat constricted with fear so badly that she couldn't even scream.

She rested by one of the booths, her hands on her knees as she caught her breath. "What a *great* place to stumble into!" she groaned. "Especially on Christmas."

She'd recently moved to Iowa for work, leaving all her family behind in Nebraska. Her flight home had been canceled because of ongoing storms, which meant she had to spend Christmas alone here in Iowa. And now she was stuck in this freakish place until the storm died down with some psychotic sign making weird demands of her. Terry found herself hoping that this was all some stupid dream, and that she'd wake up at home in Nebraska.

After several minutes without waking up, she sighed. "Maybe if I order something, I can leave."

The idea wasn't appealing, but she didn't really have any other choice. Moving slowly, she bent down to wipe the dust off the seat in the booth, thinking it would be as disgusting as the rest of the place, only to find that it was strangely clean. As Terry looked closer, she could almost make out the imprint of a body that had sat there recently.

Chills ran the length of her spine. Who had been here before her? Had they experienced the same weird things she was experiencing? What had happened to the person?

Swallowing hard, she sat down on the very edge of the seat, not letting her back touch the rear part of the seat. Terry began shivering as she wondered again why the seat looked as if it had recently been sat on. The menu was made of white paper and inscribed at the top of the cover with green lettering.

The Despicable Diner

Terry wrinkled her nose. "They got that mostly right. Should be *The Disgusting Diner*."

Turning the page, she scanned the breakfast menu, blinking a couple times when she came across an entry reading *Pamcakes with Syrup.*

"That can't be right. Someone must have made a typo."

Thinking that since it was Christmas, she might as well order a dessert, she flipped over to the dessert page. There were the usual cakes and pies, but she also found an entry called *Henry's Hearty Milk-shake.*

Something about the item sounded a little ominous. Terry felt that quaking sort of chill again and wondered if she was going to be sick. When she looked up, the stupid sign was right next to the booth, making her jump again.

"Why do you keep following me around?" she snapped, leaning as far away from the sign as she could. The sign had changed again, now reading ORDER NOW. LAST CHANCE. Did.. did the sign *change?*

Scooting as close to the wall as possible, she turned the pages of the menu back to the sandwiches, then the dinner plates. Everything sounded weird or out of place for a diner, except for one entry. She read the entry just as she heard the kitchen door begin to creak open...

Jacob's Country Fried Chicken Thighs.

Printed in the USA
CPSIA information can be obtained
at www.ICGtesting.com
CBHW032102280624
10819CB00015B/491